Enid Blyton

NAUGHTY AMELIA JANE!

More Enid Blyton published by Dean

Enid Blyton

Naughty Amelia Jane!

DEAN

EGMONT

We bring stories to life

First published in Great Britain 1939 by Newnes
This edition published 2005 by Dean,
an imprint of Egmont Books Limited.
239 Kensington High Street, London W8 6SA

Text copyright © 1939 Enid Blyton Limited.
Illustrations copyright © 2005 Enid Blyton Limited.
Illustrations by Deborah Allwright

Enid Blyton's signature is a registered
trademark of Enid Blyton Limited.
A Chorion company

ISBN 0 6035 6190 X

1 3 5 7 9 10 8 6 4 2

A CIP catalogue record for this title is available from the British Library

Printed and bound in Singapore

Contents

Naughty Amelia Jane

The toys in the nursery were very
friendly with the small pixies who lived
in the bushes below the nursery
window. The pixies had no wings, but
they managed to climb up the tall pear
tree and get in at the window whenever
it was open. So you can guess that the
toys and the pixies had many a good
game!

There was one very naughty toy, who often made the others really angry. This was Amelia Jane, a big, long-legged doll with an ugly face, a bright red frock, and yellow hair. She hadn't come from a shop, like the others, but had been made at home. Shop-toys nearly always have good manners, and know how to behave themselves – but Amelia Jane, not being a shop-toy, had no manners at all, and didn't care what she said or did!

Once she poured a jug of milk down Tom the toy soldier's neck, and that made him wet and uncomfortable for two days. Another time she threw a woollen ball up so high that it went into the goldfish globe, and made the

poor goldfish jump almost out of his
skin. Then, when the teddy bear
climbed up to get the ball out of the
water, Amelia Jane climbed up behind

3

him, gave him a push – and there was the poor bear, spluttering away in the water, and trying his hardest to swim, whilst the goldfish darted at him in fury.

Dear dear, how Amelia Jane laughed, and how all the other toys shouted at her! Whatever would she do next?

The next thing she did was to catch a bee in a matchbox, and then, when the sailor doll needed matches, she gave him the matchbox, pretending that there were matches inside. You can

imagine how scared he was when a bee
flew out and stung him on the nose!

'Amelia Jane, you are a perfect
nuisance,' said the toys angrily. 'Can't
you settle down and be good like us?
One day you will do something that will
get us all into trouble!'

'Pooh!' said Amelia Jane rudely.
'I shan't!'

But she did do
something very
naughty indeed
the next
time.

She was
hunting about in
Nanny's work-basket for a
thimble to play with, when
she came across Nanny's
scissors. Ho! Now she
could have a fine game of
cutting!

So she took the
scissors and began
to snip-snip-snip
everything! The
other toys were
sitting in a corner playing a game
of snap, and they didn't notice at first
what Amelia Jane was doing. They
wouldn't let Amelia play snap with
them because she said 'Snap!' when it
wasn't, and took away all their cards.

So Amelia Jane had a lovely time all by herself. She snipped a hole in the curtains, and then she snipped another! Then she went to the hearth-rug and cut a whole corner off that! Then she found Nanny's handkerchief on the floor, and do you know, she cut it into twenty-two tiny pieces! It was one of Nanny's best hankies too, with a pretty lace edge. But Amelia Jane didn't care about that!

Then she went to the carpet and began to snip little bits of it here and there. The carpet was a green one with red roses, and wherever Amelia could see a rose, she snipped! Wasn't it dreadful of her?

The toys took no notice. They were having such a lovely game. Amelia grew cross with them for being happy without her. So what do you suppose she did? She went up behind the pink rabbit and snipped his tail off!

Goodness! You should have seen

how he jumped!

'Ooooooh!' he yelled. 'She's snipped my tail off! Look! Oh, the wicked, wicked doll!'

'And look what else she's done!' cried the toys in horror, pointing to the spoilt hanky, the snipped rug, and the cut carpet. 'And look, she's spoilt the curtains too. Oh, what trouble we shall get into! Nanny will know it must be the toys, and she will throw us all into the dustbin! Oh!'

The toys stared in horror at all that the naughty doll had done. The pink rabbit cried bitterly, for he felt dreadful without a tail. Oh dear! How he would be laughed at, now that he hadn't a tail! Tom the toy soldier put his arm round him and comforted him.

'Don't worry, Bunny,' he said. 'We shall all love you just the same, even if you don't wear a tail, and look rather like a guinea-pig!'

The pink rabbit cried all the more loudly when he heard that. 'I don't want to be like a guinea-pig!' he wept. 'I want to be like a rabbit! I hate Amelia Jane! Punish her, Tom! She is a very wicked doll!'

Amelia Jane laughed. She loved doing naughty things. She liked seeing all the toys staring in horror at the mischief she had done. Ha, Ha! That would teach them to play snap without her!

'Give me those scissors,' said Tom sternly.

'Shan't!' said Amelia Jane, twirling

them round in her big hand.

'I said, "Give me those scissors!" ' ordered the toy soldier.

'I said "Shan't!" ' said Amelia Jane, 'and if you talk to me like that, Tom, I'll chop your hat into little pieces! Then you'll look horrid!'

'You naughty, wicked doll!' said Tom, in a fury. But he didn't dare to try to take the scissors away, for they had very sharp points, and he really was afraid that Amelia Jane would cut up his lovely hat. He was very proud of it, and he didn't want anything to happen to it.

'Whatever shall we do?' said the teddy bear. The toys all looked at one another in despair.

Then they heard a little scraping

noise at the window, and they saw their friends, the pixies, creeping in at the crack at the bottom.

'Hallo, Toys! You look very miserable!' said the pixies, scrambling down from the window-seat to the floor. 'What's the matter? Have you lost a pound and found a penny?'

'No,' said the toys. 'Just look here, pixies, at what Amelia Jane has done!'

'I say!' said the pixies, staring at all the damage. 'Why did you let her have scissors? And look, she still has them. You ought to take them away from her before she does any more mischief.'

'She won't let us have them,' said Tom. 'She says she will chop my hat into little pieces if I try to take them from her.'

'Oho, we'll soon see to that!' said the biggest pixie at once. 'Scissors, come to me!'

He waved his little gold wand – and immediately the scissors flew out of Amelia Jane's hand and went to the pixie. He caught them and gave them to Tom.

'Oh, thank you,' said the toys gratefully. 'I suppose you couldn't help us to mend all these dreadful holes and slits that Amelia has made?'

'Oh yes, I think so,' said the biggest pixie. 'We'll just go and get our needles and thread, and come back to help you. We'll sew everything so that you won't see even a tiny stitch! We are very clever at stitching, you know. Once we sewed all the petals on a daisy that had lost hers in a rainstorm – and you really couldn't see that they were not growing! As for that handkerchief, we'll use a bit of magic for that, and all the bits will join together so that Nanny will never know it has been cut!'

The pixies fetched their needles and thread, and soon they were sitting on the carpet and on the rug, mending all the slits and cuts, and two of them mended the curtains. Then the biggest pixie put a spell into his needle and sewed on the bunny's tail again. It didn't hurt a bit because of the spell. The bunny was so grateful.

The handkerchief was mended too – and everything was put right.

'There!' said the pixies, in delight. 'We've done all we can!'

'We can't thank you enough!' said the toys. 'You may be sure that if ever we can help you in return we will!'

'As for Amelia Jane,' said the biggest pixie, 'I should keep her a prisoner in the toy-cupboard until she says she is sorry and won't be naughty any more. Here is a spell that will keep her there!'

Tom took the spell. It was in a little box, and when it was taken out and blown over Amelia, she had to stay where she was put. The toys surrounded the naughty doll, pushed her into the cupboard, and then blew the spell at her. She couldn't move her legs! There she had to stay!

At first she was very angry. Then she was frightened, and begged to be set free. She saw the toys going happily about their play, and she wanted to join them. It was dreadfully dull in the toy-cupboard all alone except for a box of bricks that never said a word.

'I'm sorry, Toys! Do set me free!' begged Amelia Jane. 'I will try very hard not to be naughty any more.'

'If we could be sure you would do good things and not naughty ones, *we would* set you free,' said Tom. 'But we don't trust you. You have never done a good or brave thing all the time you have been with us.'

Amelia Jane was just going to answer him when there came a tapping at the window. The toys looked up. A

small red robin was there. He looked
most excited.

'What is it?' shouted the toys,
swarming up to the window-seat.

'It's the pixies!' said the robin.
'They have been attacked by the
goblins! They have hidden in the old
hollow tree, but the goblins are cutting
it down! Can you rescue them?'

'How?' said Tom, upset and
bothered to hear such bad news.

'I don't know,' said the robin.
'You'll have to think of something –
but hurry, because at any moment the
goblins may get them!'

He flew off, and the toys crowded
together, all talking at once.

'Toys, Toys, I have a plan!' cried
Amelia Jane from the cupboard. 'Let

me fly the toy aeroplane out of the window. It will frighten the goblins terribly, and they are sure to run away. Then, before they come back, the pixies can get into the aeroplane and I'll fly it safely back here!'

'All right!' shouted the toys, excited. 'It's a good idea. Set her free, Tom.'

So Amelia Jane was set free. The aeroplane was run up to her, and she got in. Rr-rr-rr-rr-rr! It shot up into the air and out of the window. How exciting it was! Amelia was a bit afraid of falling out, but she managed to guide the aeroplane to the hollow tree. Then down she flew – and all the little goblins who were cutting down the tree to get at the pixies inside, cried out in horror:

'Run! Run! The aeroplane is coming down on top of us!'

They scattered in fright. Amelia stopped the aeroplane and landed by the hollow tree. She called to the pixies:

'Pixies! Quickly! Get into my aeroplane! I've come to rescue you!'

The pixies all shot out of the hollow tree at once and clambered into the plane. When the goblins saw what was happening they gave a shout of rage and ran to the aeroplane at once – but it was too late. Rr-rr-rr-rr-rr! It rose into the air, and flew straight back to the nursery window. In two minutes the pixies were safe in the nursery with the toys, and *how* pleased they were!

'Amelia Jane has turned over a new leaf,' said the pixies, in surprise. 'Brave Amelia Jane! Thank you so much for rescuing us!'

'Don't mention it!' said Amelia. 'I am trying very hard to be good now.'

And you will be pleased to hear that she certainly *was* good for a little while, but I'm afraid it didn't last for very long!

Amelia Jane
Gets a Shock

Well, for a little while Amelia Jane was very good – and then, oh dear, she forgot all her promises, and became really naughty! The things she did!

She took a needle and cotton out of Nanny's work-basket, and sewed up the sleeves of the teddy bear's new coat when he wasn't looking. So when he went to put on his coat, he simply could *not* put his arms through the sleeves anyhow! He just couldn't find the way in – because the sleeves were sewn up! How Amelia Jane laughed to see him!

The next night she hid behind the curtain and began to mew like a cat. The toys were not very fond of Tibs the cat, because he sometimes chewed them. So they all stopped playing and looked round to see where Tibs was.

'I can hear him mewing!' said the teddy bear. 'He must be behind the door.'

But he wasn't. Amelia mewed again. The toys hunted all about for the cat. They even looked in the coal-scuttle, and under the hearth-rug, which made Amelia laugh till she nearly choked! She mewed again, very loudly.

'Where is that cat!' cried Tom the toy soldier, in despair. 'We've looked everywhere! Is he behind the curtain?'

'No, there's only Amelia Jane there!' said the golden-haired doll, looking. 'There's no cat.'

Well, of course, they didn't find any cat at all! And Amelia Jane didn't tell them it was she who had been mewing,

so to this day they wonder where Tibs
hid himself that night!

Then Amelia Jane saw a soda-water
siphon left in a corner of the room. She
knew how it worked, because she had
seen Nanny using one. Oh, what fun it
would be to squirt all the
toys!

She stole towards it – picked it up, and dear me, it *was* heavy! She ran at the surprised Tom, pressed down the handle – and out gushed the soda-water all over him!

'Ow! Ooh!' he shouted, in astonishment. 'What is it? What is it? Amelia Jane, you ought to be ashamed of yourself!'

But she wasn't a bit ashamed. She was just enjoying herself thoroughly! She ran after the teddy bear and soaked him with soda-water too. She squirted lots over the clockwork mouse, and made him so wet that for two days his clockwork went wrong, and he couldn't be wound up. She squirted the pink rabbit, and he got into the wastepaper basket and couldn't get out, which worried him very much, because he was so afraid that Jane, the cleaner, would throw him away the next day! But she didn't, which was very lucky.

'Amelia Jane is up to her tricks again,' said the clockwork clown, frowning. 'We shall have no peace at all. What shall we do?'

'Take away her key!' said the clockwork mouse.

'She hasn't one, silly!' said Tom.

'Lock her in the cupboard!' said the teddy bear.

'She knows how to undo it from the inside,' said the pink rabbit gloomily.

Nobody spoke for a whole minute. They were all thinking hard.

Then the clockwork clown gave a

little laugh. 'I know!' he said. 'I've thought of an idea. It's quite simple, but it might work.'

'What?' cried everyone.

'Let's polish Amelia Jane's shoes underneath and make them very, very slippery,' said the clown. 'Then, if she begins to run after us with soda-water siphons or things like that, down she'll go!'

'But she won't like that,' said the golden-haired doll, who was rather tender-hearted.

'Well, *we* don't like the tricks she plays on *us*!' said Tom. 'We'll do it, Clown! When she next takes her shoes off we'll polish them underneath till they are as slippery as glass!'

The very next night Amelia Jane

took off her shoes because she said her feet were hot. She put the shoes into a corner and then danced round the nursery in her stockinged feet, enjoying herself. The clown picked up the shoes and ran away to the back of the toy-cupboard with them. He had a tiny duster there, and a little bit of polish he had taken out of Jane's polish jar when the nursery had been cleaned out. Aha, Amelia Jane, you'll be sorry for all your tricks!

The clown polished and rubbed, rubbed and polished. The soles of the shoes shone. They were as slippery as could be! The clown put them back and waited for Amelia Jane to put them on. This she very soon did, for she had stepped on a pin and pricked

her foot! As she put her
shoes on, she thought out
a naughty trick!

I'll run after all the toys
with that pin I trod on! she
thought. Oooh! That will make
them rush away into all the
corners! What fun it will be to
frighten them!

She buttoned her shoes and took
the nasty long pin into her
hand. Then she
stood up and
looked round,
her naughty eyes
gleaming. I'll run
after that fat little
teddy bear! she
thought. So

30

off she went, straight at the teddy bear, holding the pin out in front of her.

'Amelia Jane, put that pin down!' shouted the teddy bear in fright – but before Amelia Jane had taken three steps, her very, very slippery shoes slid along the ground and down she fell, bumpity-bump! She *was* so surprised!

Up she got again and took a few more steps towards the teddy bear – but her shoes slipped and down she fell! Bumpity-bump! She hit her head on the fender!

'What's the matter with the carpet?' cried Amelia Jane in a rage. 'It keeps making me fall down!'

'Ha ha! ho ho!' laughed the toys. 'Perhaps there is slippery magic about, Amelia Jane!'

'Oh, I believe you toys have something to do with it!' shouted the angry doll. Up she got and took the pin in her hand again. 'I'll show you what happens to people who put slippery magic on the floor! Here comes my pin!'

She tried to run at Tom, who was laughing so much that the tears ran all down his face. But down she went again, bumpity-bump – and oh my, the pin stuck into her knee! Yes, it really did – she fell on it!

How Amelia Jane squealed! How Amelia Jane wept! 'Oh, the horrid pin! Oh, how it hurts!' she cried.

'Well, Amelia Jane, it serves you right,' said the pink rabbit. 'You were going to prick *us* with that pin and now it's pricked *you*! You know how it feels!'

Amelia Jane threw the pin away in a rage. The clown picked it up and flung it into the fire! He wasn't going to have pins about the nursery!

Amelia Jane got up again. 'I'm going to bandage my knee where the pin pricked it,' she said. She ran to the toy cupboard – but before she was halfway there, her slippery shoes slid away beneath her – and down she sat with a dreadful bumpity-bumpity-bump!

The toys laughed. Amelia Jane cried bitterly. The golden-haired doll felt sorry for her. 'Don't cry any more, Amelia Jane,' she said. 'Take your shoes off and you won't fall again. We played a trick on you – but you can't complain because you have so often tricked *us*! You should not play jokes on other people if you can't take a joke yourself!'

Amelia Jane took her shoes off. She saw how the clown had polished them underneath, and she went very red. She knew quite well she could not grumble if people were unkind – because she too had been unkind.

'I'll try and be good, Toys,' she said at last. 'It's difficult for me, because I'm not a shop-toy like you, so I haven't learnt good manners and nice ways. But I may be good one day!'

The toys thought it was nice of her to say all that. The golden-haired doll

came to help her bandage her knee.
The clown put a bandage round her
head where she had bumped it. She
looked so funny that they didn't know

whether to laugh or cry at her.

Amelia Jane did enjoy being fussed!
She was as nice as could be to the toys
– but oh dear, oh dear, I do somehow
feel perfectly certain that she can't be
good for long!

Amelia Jane at the Sea

Once it happened that Amelia Jane, the big, naughty doll, was taken down to the seaside with some of the other toys. The clockwork clown went, the brown teddy bear, Tom the toy soldier, and the golden-haired doll. They went in the car with the children, and they were all most excited.

'I shall dig in the sand and throw it

over everybody!' said naughty Amelia Jane. 'And I shall get my pail and fill it full of water and pour it down Tom's neck! Ho, won't he jump!'

'You'll do nothing of the sort, Amelia Jane,' said Tom at once. 'You know how often you've promised to be good. Well, just you remember your promise.'

'And I shall push the clockwork clown into a

rock-pool and make him sit down there with all his clothes on,' said Amelia Jane, with a naughty giggle.

'You mustn't!' cried the clown, in alarm. 'If you do that, my clockwork will get rusty and I shan't wind up properly – then I won't be able to walk any more, or turn head-over-heels!'

The children often took the toys down to the beach with them. After dinner the children went to have a rest, and the toys were left in a sheltered corner of the beach. No one ever came there, so the children knew they were quite safe. And it was whilst the toys were left alone there that Amelia Jane behaved so very badly. She did all she said she would, and more too.

She threw sand all over the golden-haired doll, and it went into her eyes dreadfully. She cried, and Tom had to find his handkerchief and comfort her. Whilst he was patting the doll on the back, and wiping the sand out of her eyes, Amelia Jane was filling her pail from a pool.

She crept up behind Tom and tipped the pail of cold sea-water all down his neck!

'Ooooo-ow-oooo!' yelled Tom, jumping about twelve

centimetres into the air with fright. 'You wicked doll, Amelia Jane! I told you not to do that!'

Amelia Jane thought it was such a funny joke that she rolled over and over on the sand, laughing. The clockwork clown, who had seen all that had happened, remembered what she had said she would do to him, and he ran away to hide. He really was dreadfully afraid Amelia Jane would push him into a pool. Amelia looked for him. He had hidden himself under a clump of seaweed, so she couldn't see him – but she saw the brown teddy bear!

He was walking round the edge of a deep pool, looking at the crabs there. Amelia Jane crept up behind him. She gave him a push – SPLASH! The teddy landed in the pool and sat right down in the water.

'Oooooo-ow-ooooo!' he gasped, his mouth full of salty water. Amelia Jane laughed till the tears ran down her face.

'You are very naughty and

unkind,' said the clockwork clown, poking his head out of the seaweed nearby. 'You are a most dreadful doll. Hi, Tom, come and help me push Amelia Jane into the water!'

'I shan't let you!' said Amelia Jane, at once. 'I shall paddle out to sea and sit on that rock over there. I am bigger than any of you, and I can get through the deep water easily. You won't be able to follow me. I shall be quite safe. Ha ha to you, clockwork clown!'

Amelia Jane had no shoes or socks on. She lifted up her red skirt and stepped into the waves. She waded out towards the big, big rock that showed itself some way out. It was covered with green seaweed. The teddy shook the water from his fur and ran after Amelia, splashing through the waves. But he was afraid of getting drowned, and he soon came back. Amelia was a very big doll, so she could easily get to the rock. The water did not come to more than her knees.

She reached the rock and climbed up. She waved to the others.

'I'm the king of the castle!' she shouted, dancing on the rock. 'You can't get me! I shall stay here and have a nice nap!'

She lay down on the soft green seaweed. The hot sun had dried it well. It was like a soft bed.

Amelia fell asleep. When the children came out to play, they didn't miss her. They had new spades and they wanted to dig a big castle.

They took no notice of any of the other toys, and didn't even see how wet the teddy bear was. They dug and dug and dug.

They had tea on the beach and then they dug again. When it was time to go home they collected their toys and set off up the beach. They had the clockwork clown, the bear, the toy soldier and the golden-haired doll – but they didn't have Amelia Jane. They had forgotten all about her.

And what about Amelia Jane? She was still asleep on the rock! The tide was now coming in – and it crept higher and higher over the rock. Soon it would reach Amelia's toes. Soon a big wave would break right over the rock on top of Amelia – and then what would happen to her?

Amelia woke up. She sat up on the rock and looked round. When she saw how the tide was coming in, she was in a dreadful fright. The water was too deep to paddle through now. She couldn't swim. Oh dear!

Amelia Jane stood and yelled for help. 'Save me, somebody!' she cried. 'Save me!' But there was no one to save her. Poor Amelia Jane!

The other toys were sitting on a shelf, watching the children go to bed. Nobody thought of Amelia Jane. They were only too glad to forget her.

But when the children were safely in bed, Tom the toy soldier suddenly looked round – and saw no Amelia. For a moment he wondered where she was – and then he remembered! She had been left on the rock – and the tide was coming in. Ooooo!

'I say, Toys,' said Tom, 'Amelia Jane's on the rock – and the sea will soon cover it right over!'

Now you might think that the clown, the golden-haired doll, and Tom would say, 'And serve Amelia right!' – but they didn't. They all looked at one another in alarm. Amelia was naughty – and she had played tricks on them – but they could not let anything horrid happen to her.

'What can we do?' asked the clown. He got down from the shelf and ran to the window. From there he could quite well see the rock on which Amelia stood, shouting for help.

'We must save her!' said the golden-haired doll.

'But how?' asked Tom.

'I know!' said the clown suddenly. 'We will take the children's toy ship – and sail it to the rock. We shall just get there in time. Hurry!'

The toy soldier and the clown caught hold of the toy ship, which lay on the floor. They ran out of the door with the golden-haired doll, and tore down to the beach. They put the boat into the water.

Tom got in. The golden-haired doll got in. The clockwork clown pushed off, and then jumped in himself. Tom arranged the white sails so that the wind filled them. The clown took the rudder and guided the little ship.

The tide was coming in fast. It was a long, long way now to the rock. Amelia Jane was very frightened. A big wave had washed right over the rock and had wetted her to the waist. Amelia was afraid that the next one would wash her right off the rock into the big sea.

'Help! Help!' she shouted, as another big wave came over the rock. Amelia held on to some seaweed. The sea wetted her right up to her shoulders. Oooh! It was so cold! She knew now how cold Tom must have felt when she poured water down his neck that morning!

'We're coming, Amelia Jane; we're coming!' shouted the toys. Amelia

Jane heard them.

She looked over the waves and saw the three toys in the sailing-ship. It bobbed up and down as it came, for the sea was quite rough.

'Oh, you good creatures!' sobbed Amelia Jane. 'I don't deserve to be rescued – I was so unkind to you – but oh, I'm *so* glad to see you!'

The ship sailed quite near to the rock. The clown was careful not to let it strike the rock – for that would mean a wreck. 'Jump, Amelia, jump into the ship!' he called. 'We can't come any nearer!'

Amelia Jane jumped. It was a good
jump. She landed right in the middle of
the boat. It swayed about, and then as
the clown turned it into the wind, the
sails filled and the little ship sailed
towards the shore
again.

'You'll soon
be safe
home,' said

the golden-haired doll kindly. 'Don't cry, Amelia Jane.'

'I won't tease you any more, any of you,' wept Amelia. 'It was so kind of you to remember I was on the rock and come to rescue me. Thank you ever and ever so much.'

The ship reached the sand. Tom jumped out and pulled it in. The golden-haired doll jumped out and helped poor, wet, cold Amelia Jane out. The clown jumped out last of all – and then they carried the ship back to the nursery again.

Tom took Amelia Jane down to the kitchen fire and dried her. Then back to the nursery they went, and soon fell asleep after their exciting day.

And was Amelia Jane kinder to the

toys after that? Yes, very much kinder, all the time they were away at the sea. But alas! When they went back home again, Amelia Jane forgot all her good ways. Read on and you will see!

Amelia Jane and the Cowboy Doll

Now one day a funny little doll came to stay with the toys in the nursery. He was a cowboy doll. He didn't belong to the children who owned the nursery, he was just lent to them for a few days.

He was dressed in shaggy trousers, leather tunic, and a cowboy hat. He was very smart indeed, and the other toys were a bit afraid of him.

He could ride the old wooden
horse, and made it gallop as fast as
could be round and round the nursery!
Once he even climbed up on to the big
rocking-horse and made it rock so fast
that the horse hrrumphed in surprise,
and Nanny came running in to see

what all the noise was about!

The cowboy doll only just had time to hop off the horse and lie down on the floor, where he had been put by the children!

Another thing he could do was rather marvellous. He had a long rope, and he could lasso anything with it that he liked! The toys would say to him, 'Lasso that tree on the toy farm, Cowboy doll!' And he would quickly throw his looped rope, and the end would neatly curl round the tree and topple it over!

He would lasso anything, even a pin stuck in the floor. And then, of course, Amelia Jane began to tell him naughty things to do!

'Cowboy doll, do lasso the

clockwork mouse!' she whispered. 'Oh do! Look, he is over there, sniffing at that brick!'

The cowboy doll grinned. He had a most wicked face. He threw his rope neatly, and the loop at the end dropped right over the mouse's head – click!

The mouse gave a squeak of surprise and tried to run away, but the rope held him tight! He was very frightened.

'You shouldn't tell the cowboy doll to do that, Amelia Jane,' said Tom crossly. 'Why *must* you always get into mischief? Go and untie the mouse, quickly.'

'You go, Tom,' said Amelia Jane, giggling as she thought of more mischief. 'You are better at knots than I am!'

Well, the mouse was squealing so loudly that Tom really thought he had better go and help. So off he went, and Amelia Jane nudged the cowboy doll and whispered to him:

'Where's your other rope? Lasso Tom! He will get such a shock!'

So when Tom was bending over the mouse, trying to undo the loop of rope round him, there came a whizzing noise through the air, and another rope fell neatly right round Tom's waist – click! It pinned his arms to his sides and he couldn't move! What a shock he got!

'You're my prisoner, Tom!' grinned the cowboy doll. 'Come over here!'

'I won't!' scowled Tom. 'Let me go!'

But he had to walk over to the cowboy doll and Amelia Jane because the cowboy pulled hard at the rope, and Tom had to come with it! He was so angry!

Amelia Jane thought lassoing was a lovely thing to do. She wanted to learn, and the cowboy doll said he would teach her.

'No, you are not to teach her,' said the golden-haired doll sharply. 'She is quite naughty enough without learning any more tricks. You are NOT to teach her!'

But the cowboy doll was not used to obeying other people, so he took no notice at all. He began to teach

Amelia Jane, and she tried very hard to learn.

Soon she could throw a rope wonderfully well, and then, what a time the poor toys had! They never knew when a rope was going to come whizzing through the air after them, falling over their heads and shoulders! It was most worrying.

Amelia Jane practised hard, but she could not get quite so good at it as the cowboy doll.

Once she sent the rope flying through the air to catch

the teddy bear as he walked along, and
she missed him and got the rope round
the chimney of the dolls' house.

Of course, she pulled too hard, and
the chimney came off and fell on top of
the bear's head. He was very cross
indeed, and threw the chimney at
Amelia Jane. She threw it back, and it

almost hit the nursery cat on the nose. He was most surprised, and looked as if he would eat Amelia Jane. So she ran into the cupboard till the cat had gone down to the kitchen for his dinner.

The toys made her climb up to the dolls' house roof and put the chimney on again. She didn't like that at all, but she had to do it. But even then she wouldn't stop lassoing things.

She lassoed the humming-top when it was spinning and made it fall down in a fright. She threw her rope at a cow in the farmyard, but caught the farmer himself and jerked him so high in the air that he really thought he was flying. He came down in the coal-scuttle and was very angry about it.

He told all his cows to go and bite
Amelia Jane, and she had to climb up
on to a shelf out of their way.

Another time she was very
naughty indeed. She thought she
would lasso Mister Noah, who lived in
the wooden ark, and give him a shock.
He didn't like Amelia Jane, and
wouldn't even say good morning to
her when he met her. So Amelia
waited for him to come out with all his
animals.

'I'll lasso him now!' she whispered
to the cowboy doll, with a grin.
'Watch me!'

She sent the rope through the air –
whizz! But she missed Mister Noah,
and the rope fell neatly round two
tigers and two bears! How they roared

and growled! They bit through the rope
in a twinkling, left the line of animals,
and tore over to where Amelia was
standing with the cowboy doll.

The bears bit the cowboy doll's
shaggy trousers so hard that they made

a hole in them. The tigers scratched
Amelia Jane on her legs, and you
should have heard her yell!

'It serves you right,' said Tom, who had been watching. 'We've told you ever so many times not to keep lassoing people.'

So for a little while Amelia Jane was good, but then something happened that made her bad again.

Somebody left a bag of sweets on the nursery mantelpiece. They belonged to one of the children, and Nanny had put them there. Amelia Jane saw them and looked longingly at them, for she loved eating lots of sweets and chocolates.

How could she possibly get those sweets? She looked up at the mantelpiece and thought hard. The clock ticked away there. The goldfish globe winked back. It stood on the mantelpiece too, and was full of little black tadpoles that the children had found in the ponds. The china cat stood there too, watching the tadpoles wriggling about. And just by the cat was that bag of sweets.

'Oh, I know how I can get them!' said Amelia suddenly. 'I can lasso them with the cowboy's rope! Cowboy doll, where are you? Will you lend me your rope for a moment?'

The cowboy doll untied it. He always kept it tied round his waist. He gave it to Amelia Jane and asked her what she wanted it for.

'I'm going to lasso that bag of sweets on the mantelpiece and get it down here!' said naughty Amelia. 'Then we'll share the sweets, Cowboy doll!'

'You'd better let *me* do the lassoing,' said the cowboy. 'You'll only go and lasso the cat or the clock, Amelia Jane!'

'No, *I* want to do it,' said Amelia. She looked up at the mantelpiece and swung the rope carefully. Whizz! It flew up to the mantelpiece! It missed the bag of sweets. It missed the clock. It just missed the china cat, but it caught the goldfish bowl! It fell neatly round it. The rope was tight – it pulled at the bowl – it toppled it over!

The watching toys gave a shriek! The water poured out of the bowl – all over Amelia and the cowboy doll, who were just underneath! Tadpoles fell down their necks and flopped on to the floor! The bowl fell off too, and all the toys thought it would smash on the floor.

But no! It was too clever for that! It fell on to Amelia Jane's head, and there she stood, wet through, with the glass bowl on her head like an extra big hat!

Well, really, the toys simply couldn't *help* laughing! She looked too funny, and the cowboy doll, too, was soaked from head to foot. He was trying to get a tadpole which had fallen down his back and was tickling him dreadfully.

'Don't stand there laughing like this,' said Tom suddenly. 'Those tadpoles will die out of water. Quick, get something to put them into.'

The toys looked round for something but all they could think of was Amelia Jane's teacup. She was a big doll, so she had a very big cup. The toys put some water in it and then picked up the poor wriggling tadpoles. They found the one down the cowboy's neck, and took two from Amelia's neck as well. Dear, dear, what an excitement there was!

'What do you want to bother with silly tadpoles for, when Amelia Jane and I are all wet through!' cried the cowboy doll crossly. 'Please dry us.'

'It is more important to save the tadpoles than to bother about *you*,' said the clown. 'You can dry yourselves. It was your own fault that all this happened. Amelia Jane had no right to try and lasso sweets that didn't belong to her!'

Amelia squeezed out of her wet things and took the bowl off her head. It was rather a tight fit, and at first she thought she might have to wear the bowl all her life! That did give her a shock. She stood by the fire and tried to dry herself. She felt very cold and sad. The cowboy doll was wet too, and very angry.

'You *are* silly,' he said to Amelia Jane. 'Why didn't you let me do the lassoing? I could have got the bag of sweets then, but all we got was cold water and tadpoles!'

Amelia Jane said nothing, but dear me, when she found that her teacup was full of swimming tadpoles she was horrified.

'How can I ever drink out of my nice cup again?' she wept. 'It will be all tadpoley.'

'Amelia Jane, stop being silly,' said Tom sternly. 'You have made enough mischief without being stupid too. What do you suppose Nanny will say when she finds the tadpoles upset and the bowl on the rug?'

Nanny said a lot. She simply could *not* understand what had happened! At first she thought it was the cat who had done it. But no, Tibs had been in the kitchen all the time. And then she caught sight of the cowboy doll who was standing in a corner, still very wet.

'I believe it's you, with your lasso, you naughty doll!' she said. 'Back you go to your own home!'

'Perhaps Amelia Jane will be good now that the cowboy doll has gone,' said the teddy to the clown. But I don't expect she will – do you?

Amelia Jane and the Plasticine

Now Amelia Jane had been good for a long time – so good that the golden-haired doll really wondered if Amelia was ill. But she wasn't ill; as the clown said, 'She was just boiling up for some more mischief!'

Amelia Jane had found the box of plasticine in the cupboard, and every night she played with the plasticine. She sat in a corner by herself, and the other toys took no notice of her at all. Amelia Jane was clever with the plasticine – she could make flowers and shells and tables and chairs and all kinds of things, just as you can.

And then, of course, naughty ideas began to come into her mind. She had heard the teddy bear complaining that he had no tail. Suppose she made him one and stuck it on when he was asleep? He would think he had grown a tail, and what fun it would be to see him walking about proudly, showing off his beautiful new tail! What would he say when it came off?

Amelia Jane made a beautiful long tail of plasticine. It was brown to match the teddy bear's fur, and it had some

pretty little blue spots here and there.
Amelia Jane made some marks on it to
make it look furry. It was finished at
last. Amelia Jane grinned to herself and
waited till she saw the teddy bear
asleep in a corner.

Then she crept up to him with the
plasticine tail. Nobody was about.

Amelia Jane quickly pressed one end of the tail on to the teddy bear's back. It stuck nicely. Then the naughty doll ran back to her place in the cupboard.

Presently the clockwork clown walked along to talk to the bear. He saw the tail, and he stared as if he couldn't believe his eyes!

'Hie, Teddy, Teddy, wake up!' he shouted in excitement. 'You've grown a fine tail! You have really!'

The teddy woke up with a jump. When he saw his new tail, curling round him like a cat's, he was so surprised that he couldn't say a word at first. Then he got up and bent himself over to have a look at it.

'A tail at last!' he said. 'A real tail! I always thought I might grow one, and now I have!'

'Tom, come and look at Teddy's beautiful new tail!' cried the clown. 'Do come! It's a fine one!'

Tom came, and the golden-haired doll – and Amelia went too.

'It's magnificent,' said Tom.

'It makes you look really handsome, Teddy,' said the golden-haired doll.

'How clever of you to grow it all by yourself!' said naughty Amelia Jane.

'Wasn't it clever of me!' said Teddy proudly, and he walked about showing his new tail to everyone. The clockwork mouse loved it, and the yellow duck said it was the longest she had ever seen. The bear was so happy that his boot-button eyes shone like lamps.

Not long afterwards the toys all sat down together to have cups of cocoa which the clockwork mouse had made for them on the stove in the dolls' house. Amelia Jane sat down beside the teddy – and whatever do you suppose she did? When the others were not looking she took hold of the bear's plasticine tail and with her clever fingers she made the end of it into a snake's head! Fancy that! It looked exactly like a snake now, with its mouth open and two little holes for eyes!

Tom saw it first and gave a shriek! 'Oooh! Look! Your tail has turned into a snake, Teddy!'

The bear looked down in alarm – and when he saw the snake's head on

the end of his tail he jumped up with a
yell.

'Oh! Go away, snake, go away!' he
shouted, and he ran to the other side of
the room. But, of course, his tail

followed him,
for it was
stuck on to
him – and it
looked as if
the snake
was running
after him
backwards!

Poor Teddy! He was so frightened. He didn't like snakes at all, and to have his new tail turning into one seemed very dreadful to him.

Well, Amelia Jane laughed till she cried. It seemed funny to her to see the teddy bear rushing about with a snake-tail! The toys thought her very unkind to laugh, and the golden-haired doll shouted at her. But as

Amelia Jane could shout twice as hard, that wasn't much good!

'Take your tail off, silly, if you're afraid of it!' called Amelia Jane.

'How can you take off a thing that's growing on you, stupid!' yelled back the teddy.

Amelia Jane ran to the bear and jerked at his tail. It came off quite easily, of course, for it was only plasticine. She threw it out of the window. The toys looked on in surprise. Then they all cheered Amelia.

'How brave of you, Amelia Jane! How good of you to do that! Did it hurt, Teddy?'

'Not a bit,' said Teddy, in surprise. 'Oh, thank you, Amelia Jane. The snake might have bitten you. You are very brave.'

Amelia Jane didn't tell the toys that the tail had only been plasticine made by herself. No – the naughty doll said nothing at all, but let the toys make a fuss of her.

I'll think of another plasticine trick, she thought gleefully. And, as you can guess, it wasn't very long before she did!

She made a set of nice little chairs, all with seats and backs and four neat little legs. Then she went to the paintbox and got the red paint. She painted those little chairs a bright red, and really, they looked simply lovely when she had finished. But, of course, you couldn't sit down on them because they were only made of plasticine and would crumple up at once!

But they didn't look as if they were made of plasticine when they were bright red. They looked like wooden chairs. Amelia Jane set them all out neatly in the middle of the floor.

'What are those chairs for?' asked Tom, in surprise.

'I'm going to have a party,' said Amelia Jane, and she got a table from the dolls' house. Then she called to the toys, 'Do come and join my party. The cakes haven't come yet but they'll be here soon. Just come and sit down and wait a while, Toys!'

The toys were pleased, for they loved any sort of a party. They came

running over to Amelia Jane. Even the
clockwork mouse came, and so did the
old blue rabbit who had only one eye
and no whiskers at all.

'Do sit down,' said Amelia, waving
her hand to the red chairs. 'I hope
there are enough seats for you all!'

Everyone sat down – but oh, what
a shock they got! Tom's chair sank
down at once, all its
legs broken! He
landed with such a
bump on the
ground! The
golden-
haired
doll's
chair

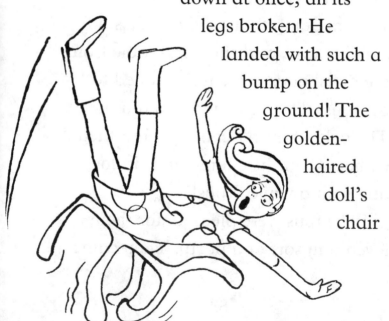

tipped over backwards, and she bumped her head, and sat so hard on the plasticine that it stuck to her pretty blue frock. The clockwork mouse's chair crumpled up and he fell off and lost his key.

One by one all the red chairs gave way and tipped out the surprised toys. The clown didn't know what was happening and he clutched the back of his chair so hard that he squeezed up the plasticine it was made of and got it all over his arms! What a shock for him!

Amelia Jane thought it was so funny! She laughed and laughed and laughed.

'It isn't funny,' said Tom angrily. 'Is this a trick instead of a party?'

'Yes,' said Amelia Jane. 'Oh, Tom you did look funny tumbling on to the floor!'

'I suppose there are no cakes coming after all,' said the clown fiercely. 'And I suppose too that it was you who stuck on the teddy bear's tail, and made it of plasticine! You are a wicked doll and you deserve to be frightened yourself!'

'Oh, you can't frighten me!' said Amelia Jane. 'I'm not afraid of anything!'

But she was, you know – she was afraid of beetles! The toys knew this, and they made up their minds to punish her! They went to the plasticine box, and the clown, who was clever with his fingers, made lots of big beetles, all with feelers on their heads and six legs under their bodies! The clown painted them black.

'This isn't a very kind thing to do,' said the clown, as he finished the last beetle, 'but really, Amelia Jane is so naughty that we must teach her a lesson. Where is she?'

'In the toy-cupboard, reading,' said the mouse. The clown took up the beetles and put them here and there on the floor. Then he called Amelia Jane.

'Amelia, Amelia, come quickly!'

Amelia Jane put down her

book and rushed out of the cupboard –
but when she saw those plasticine
beetles she gave such a yell!

'Oooh! Ow! Beetles! Where have
they come from? Take them away!'

The bear had tied a bit of black
cotton to one beetle and he suddenly
jerked this. The beetle jumped, and
Amelia Jane screamed: 'It's coming
after me! It's coming after me!
Oooooooh!'

She rushed back into the toy
cupboard and crouched in the darkest
corner. And do you know, she didn't
come out of the cupboard for two days,
so the toys had a lovely time playing
together without wondering what
mischief Amelia Jane was up to!

They have taken away the beetles,

of course, but Amelia Jane doesn't know that! She'll think twice before she gets into mischief again, won't she!

Stop it, Amelia Jane!

You might think that Amelia Jane would grow out of her bad ways, but she didn't. The day soon came when she felt bad again. It was the day that the pop-gun came to the nursery. The children had bought it and had been playing with it. It was great fun.

It was a wooden gun that had a cork fitted in at the end of it. When you

pressed the trigger the cork flew out
with a pop, but it didn't go far,
because it was tied on to the gun with
a piece of string. The children set up
their wooden soldiers in a row and
shot them down – bang! – with the
pop-gun. The soldiers didn't mind,
because it was what they were made
for.

But when Amelia Jane got hold of
the pop-gun that night and began
shooting the cork at
everyone, there
was trouble!

'Stop
it, Amelia
Jane!'
shouted
the

clockwork clown angrily, when his cap flew off into the coal-scuttle, shot there by the cork.

'Stop it, Amelia Jane!' cried Tom when he got the cork in his eye.

'Stop it, Amelia Jane!' squealed the engine. 'You're making my funnel loose with that cork – it keeps hitting it!'

But do you suppose Amelia Jane stopped? Of course not! She was enjoying herself far too much!

She shot at the castle of bricks and down they all fell! She shot at everything in the toy farmyard, and trees, animals, and farmer fell over flat. She shot at the clockwork mouse and gave him such a fright that he ran into the dolls' house and hid under a bed. Nobody could get him out.

The clockwork clown called the other toys to him. 'We've got to stop Amelia Jane!' he said. 'I'm tired of all this popping. That cork doesn't do much damage but it stings all the same.'

'What about shooting Amelia Jane?' asked Tom eagerly. 'I'd like to do that.'

'Oh, she won't let that pop-gun go, you may be sure of that!' said the teddy bear.

'Well, there's a funny old gun in the cupboard that the children got out of a cracker,' said the clockwork clown. 'Why not shoot at her with that?'

'Because it doesn't shoot, silly,' said the bear. 'I've tried it heaps of times.'

'If it only made a pop it would do,' said the clown gloomily. 'We don't really want to shoot Amelia Jane – only to frighten her and make her stop popping the cork-gun at us.'

'Well, that old gun doesn't shoot and it doesn't make a pop either,' said Tom.

Then the bear had an idea. 'Listen!' he whispered, so that Amelia Jane wouldn't hear. 'I know where there is a packet of balloons! Couldn't we get them – and blow them up – and let Tom hide behind the curtain with them? Then I could hold the gun and point it at Amelia Jane – and at the same moment Tom could prick a balloon and burst it! Then it would go

– *bang*! just like a gun – and frighten
Amelia Jane!'

Everyone thought that was a
splendid idea. So Tom got the packet
of balloons and organised the toys to
blow them up. They hid behind the

curtains with the balloons. There were five. The bear found the gun and polished it up. Amelia Jane saw him and laughed.

'*That* old gun won't shoot!' she said, and she aimed the pop-gun at Teddy and shot the cork so hard that one of his ears went crooked. He was very angry.

'Oh, so you think this old gun won't shoot!' he said. 'Well, you're wrong!'

He pointed the gun at Amelia Jane – and at the same moment Tom dug a pin into one of the blown-up balloons behind the curtain.

Bang! went the balloon – and Amelia Jane gave a shriek. She really thought the gun that Teddy was holding had gone off!

'I'm shot! I'm shot!' yelled Amelia Jane in a fright. Everyone laughed. Teddy pointed the gun at the naughty doll again. Bang! went another balloon behind the curtains. Amelia Jane squealed and ran away.

'I'm shot again! I'm shot again!' she yelled. Teddy laughed so much that he nearly dropped the gun.

'Do you promise not to shoot anybody with that pop-gun again?' he said.

'No, I don't!' said Amelia Jane.

'All right then!' said Teddy, and he pointed the gun at her again. 'I'll go on shooting at *you* then.'

Bang! went a third balloon behind the curtain, and Amelia Jane screamed, 'I'm shot! I'm shot! He's shot me three times!'

Bang! went another balloon, and Bang! went the fifth balloon. Amelia Jane screamed so loudly that she quite deafened everyone. She fled into the toy-cupboard and wept bitterly.

'I won't shoot anyone any more. Here's the old pop-gun!' she cried and she threw it out of the cupboard to the teddy bear. 'Stop shooting me! I'm wounded everywhere!'

When Amelia Jane next came out of the toy-cupboard the toys stared in astonishment – for the big doll had bandaged her arms and legs and head. She did look funny!

'You shot me five times and wounded me,' said Amelia Jane in a hurt voice. 'You ought to be very sorry.'

But the toys laughed and laughed and laughed. How could she be wounded when it was only balloons that went off pop and not the gun? Oh, Amelia Jane, you are just a humbug!

Amelia Jane Up the Chimney

Into the nursery where naughty Amelia Jane lived, came a little black kitten one day. Its eyes were green, its tail was fat and long, and its little paddy-paws were like velvet.

All the toys loved the kitten at once – but Amelia Jane loved it most of all! How she cuddled it! How she fussed it!

How she stroked it from ears to tail-tip and tickled it under its soft black chin!

The kitten belonged to the housekeeper. It was a pretty, gentle little thing, and it let the toys do what they liked with it. The teddy found it a buttery crumb to nibble. The clockwork clown turned head over heels seven times running to make it laugh. Tom found the dolls' hairbrush and brushed its fur till it shone.

But Amelia Jane wanted the kitten all to herself. She pushed away the other toys, and as she was bigger than they were they fell down, flop! That was the worst of Amelia – she was always so rough!

'*I* want this kitten!' said Amelia Jane. 'Tiddles, Tiddles, purr to me, and to no one else!'

'You are very selfish, Amelia Jane,' said Tom. Amelia Jane stuck out her elbow and pushed him again. Down he went, flip-flop! You couldn't do anything with Amelia Jane when she was feeling like that.

'This kitten is mine when it comes into our nursery,' said Amelia. 'Nobody else is to play with it then.'

Well, the kitten quite enjoyed being made a fuss of by Amelia, but it did want to play with the other toys sometimes. Amelia just wouldn't let it.

She caught it and put it on her knee to stroke as soon as ever it ran over to Tom or Teddy.

And one day Amelia Jane thought she would like to dress the kitten up in clothes out of the dolls' chest-of-drawers! Quite a lot of clean dolls' clothes were kept there. It was really rather exciting to pull open the drawers and see the dear little coats and dresses, the fussy little bonnets with ribbons on, the socks and the shoes of all colours!

Amelia Jane pulled out the whole lot. She would, of course!

'Just look at that!' groaned Tom. 'Untidy creature! She'll never put those clothes back again neatly. *We* shall have to do that!'

Amelia Jane soon had all the clothes on the floor. She wondered which would fit the little black kitten. What fun to dress her up, she thought!

'This dress will fit you nicely, Tiddles,' she said, picking up a little red frock. 'Oh, you will look sweet in it. And this yellow coat will fit you, too – and this little bonnet with ribbons! Oh, what a darling kitten you will look!'

'Mee-ow,' said Tiddles, not at all liking the idea of being dressed up by Amelia Jane. 'Mee-ow! I'm off!'

She shot to the nursery door – but Amelia Jane was too quick. She reached out her hand and caught poor Tiddles. 'You come here!' she said. 'I'm going to make you look really sweet!'

Well, Tiddles had to sit and be dressed up. First Amelia put on the little red frock and did all the buttons up the back. Then she put on the yellow coat. She tied a ribbon round Tiddles' waist. Then she put the bonnet on Tiddles' little black head and tied it on firmly.

'There!' she said. 'You are now a little dolly cat! You look lovely! Look, everybody!'

Everybody came to look. They couldn't help thinking that Tiddles really did look rather sweet – but Tiddles hated it! She struggled and wriggled and tried her hardest to scrape off her bonnet. She didn't like anything over her ears. She couldn't hear properly.

'Now, you shall look at yourself in the mirror, Tiddles,' said Amelia Jane, and she carried the dressed-up kitten to the big mirror.

The kitten looked at herself – and when she saw herself looking so very strange, with a bonnet on her ears, and a coat and dress hiding her black fur, she was afraid.

'Mee-ow! It isn't me!' she said in a fright, and she rushed away to go downstairs to the housekeeper. But Amelia Jane pushed the door shut.

'You're not to go away, Tiddles,' she said. 'We want to see you walking about nicely in your new clothes.'

But that was just what Tiddles couldn't and wouldn't do! She caught sight of herself in the mirror again and ran off in terror. She was so frightened that she meant to get out of the nursery somehow! But how could she? The door was shut. The window was shut.

'Oh, where can I go-ee-ow?' mewed poor Tiddles.

Now it was summer-time, so there was no fire in the nursery grate. Tiddles leapt over the guard, and in a moment she scrabbled up the chimney and was gone!

The toys stared at one another in alarm. What would happen to Tiddles up the chimney?

'Are you all right, Tiddles?' called Tom, sticking his head up the chimney.

'No-ee-oh-ee-ow!' wailed poor Tiddles, who was more frightened than ever up the dark chimney. She didn't dare to go up and she didn't dare to go down! Poor Tiddles!

The toys turned fiercely on naughty Amelia Jane. 'It's your fault!' shouted Teddy. 'You would dress her up and frighten her, just to amuse yourself. Now what are we to do?'

'Oh-ee-ow-ee-oh!' wailed Tiddles, up the chimney.

'I know! We'll make Amelia Jane go up the chimney and fetch Tiddles!' cried Tom. 'That's what we'll do!'

'I won't go,' said Amelia Jane.

'Oh yes, you will!' said Teddy. 'Come on, everyone. Push Amelia up the chimney!'

But they couldn't get the big doll to go. She just wouldn't be pushed. Just as the toys were going to have another push at Amelia, someone opened the nursery door. It was the housekeeper!

The toys at once lay down flat on the floor and kept quite still.

'I wonder where that kitten of mine is,' said the housekeeper, looking round the nursery. 'I thought I heard her mewing up here.'

'Oh-ee-ow-ee-ow!' wailed Tiddles from the chimney. The housekeeper looked astonished. 'I believe she's up the chimney!' she said. Then someone called her from downstairs and she hurried away.

Now Amelia Jane, although she really was a very naughty doll, was feeling most uncomfortable about poor Tiddles, for she was fond of her. As soon as the housekeeper had gone she ran across to the fireplace, climbed over the guard, and looked up the chimney.

'I'm going up the chimney to

rescue
Tiddles,'
she said to
the surprised
toys. 'I'm not
going because
you tried to
push me up –
I'm going
because I don't
like Tiddles to be
frightened.'

And up the
chimney went
Amelia Jane! The
toys listened to her
scrabbling her way
up the long, dark, sooty chimney. Bits
of soot fell down and one bit hit the

teddy on the nose. 'The chimney wants sweeping,' he said.

'Looks as if Amelia is sweeping it!' said Tom, as another bit of soot rolled down.

At last Amelia Jane reached Tiddles who sat in a sooty corner, trembling. Amelia Jane put her arm round the kitten and hugged her. 'I'll help you to get down,' she said.

But dear me, that wasn't easy! Amelia Jane lost her way in the chimney, which joined all sorts of other chimneys here and there! Tiddles clung to her with all her claws and Amelia felt as if she was being pricked with twenty needles!

Now, very soon, the housekeeper came into the nursery again, and who do you suppose was with her? The sweep! Yes – the housekeeper had told him a kitten was up the chimney, and he had said he would try to sweep her out very gently.

He screwed on the handles of his big brush one after another, and the brush went higher and higher up the chimney. Amelia Jane heard it coming. She didn't know the chimney was being swept. The toys had all rushed into the cupboard when they heard the housekeeper and the sweep coming upstairs! They hadn't had time to tell her anything.

'Oooh! What's this coming up the chimney?' suddenly said Amelia, as she dimly saw something black and hairy coming nearer and nearer. She didn't know it was the sweep's round black brush! 'Oooh! It's got whiskers! It's touched me! It's pushing me!'

Poor Amelia Jane! She was just as frightened as the kitten had been when it first ran up the chimney! She couldn't get away from the brush. It lifted her and the kitten up, up, and up!

'It's caught me, it's caught me!' wept Amelia. 'I didn't know a whiskery thing lived in chimneys!'

The brush swept Amelia Jane and the kitten right out of the chimney into the air! The kitten fell to the roof on its feet, and made its way carefully down to the kitchen, where the housekeeper took off the dolls' clothes in much astonishment.

Amelia didn't fall on her *feet*, because she wasn't a cat but a doll! She slid down the roof. She hung for a moment in the gutter. She fell over the gutter – down, down, down – and into the prickly holly bush that grew just below!

'Ooh-ee-ow-ee-oh!' yelled Amelia, for the holly bush pricked her well! She scrambled out somehow and after a long time got back to the nursery.

But when she crept in at the door, what a fright she gave the toys! She was covered in soot from head to toe. Her clothes were all torn! Her face and arms were pricked and scratched!

'Oooooh!' yelled the toys and rushed to shut themselves in the cupboard. 'What is it? What is it?'

'It's me, Amelia Jane,' said Amelia, in a very small voice. 'I've come back.'

'Well, you look DREADFUL!' said Teddy, sticking his head out of the cupboard. 'For goodness' sake undress and have a bath and put on clean clothes!'

So Amelia did – but the clothes in the dolls' chest were much too small for her, and she did look funny walking about in things belonging to the baby doll!

'I shall be good in future,' said Amelia Jane. But I don't believe it, do you?

Amelia Jane
and the soap

Amelia Jane was feeling very bored. She had behaved herself for a whole week!

'But only because she hasn't been able to think of anything naughty to do,' said Tom to Teddy. 'As soon as she thinks of something she'll cheer up and be as bad as ever.'

Well, it wasn't long before Amelia

Jane did cheer up. She had thought of something.

You see, it was like this – she had gone out for a nice walk, sitting in the dolls' pram, and she had been taken into the town. Now, racing up and down the pavement were two boys on roller-skates. What a pace they went!

Amelia Jane leaned out of the pram to watch them. She thought it was a lovely game. She tried to see what the boys had on their feet, but they went so fast that Amelia Jane really didn't see what the skates were like.

How *do* they slip along so fast? she thought. I *would* like to skate like that. How I wish I could! I'd go round and round the nursery, and down the passage and back. My, wouldn't the toys stare!

Now, when Amelia Jane had an idea she just had to carry it out. So when she got back to the nursery she sat at the back of the toy-cupboard and thought hard.

'I want to skate,' she said to herself. 'I want to put something on my feet and slip along like those boys. I want to go fast! But what can I put on my feet?'

'What are you thinking so hard about?' asked the clockwork clown, poking his head in at the door.

'Never you mind,' said Amelia Jane.

'Tell me, and maybe I can help,' said the clown.

'Well, I'm trying to think of something nice and slippery,' said Amelia Jane.

'What about jelly?' said the clown.

'Don't be silly,' said Amelia.

'Well, soap,' said the clown. 'Nice wet soap! Why, the other day I got hold of some wet soap and squeezed it – and it shot out of my hand like lightning and hit Tom on the ear!'

Amelia Jane laughed. Then she stopped and thought quickly. Soap! Yes – that was really a *good* idea! If

she got two nice pieces of soap, made
them wet and slippery and tied them
under her feet, she would be able to slip
along just like those boys on skates!
Good!

'I'll try it!' said Amelia Jane. So she
ran out of the toy-cupboard and went
to the nursery basin. She climbed up

and looked to see if there was any soap there. There was – and what luck! – it had broken into two nice pieces.

'Oooh!' said Amelia, in delight. 'Just what I want!'

She turned on the tap and wetted the soap till it was so slippery she could hardly hold it. Then she climbed down with it. The toys looked at her in amazement.

'What are you going to do?' said Teddy. 'Are you going to give yourself a good wash for once?'

'Don't be rude,' said Amelia. 'You'll see in a minute what I'm going to do.'

She took off a hair-ribbon and tore it in two. Naughty Amelia! Then she tied one piece of soap under her right foot and the other piece under her left foot. The toys stared at her as if they thought she was mad.

'Amelia, that's a funny way of

washing your feet,' said Tom at last.

'I'm not washing my feet. I'm going to *skate*!' said Amelia proudly. 'Turn back the carpet, somebody. I must skate on the polished floor.'

The toys began to giggle. Really, what *would* Amelia Jane do next! Teddy and Tom turned back the carpet. Unfortunately they rolled the clockwork mouse up in it and had to unroll it again to get him out.

'Oh, do be quick!' said Amelia impatiently. 'I am simply longing to begin!'

At last the carpet was rolled right back. Amelia Jane began. She put first one foot out – slid along a little way on the soap – then put the other foot forward and slid too – and before the toys knew what she was about, there she was, skating round the nursery on her soap-skates!

How the toys laughed! Really, it was too funny to see Amelia sliding along so fast on pieces of soap!

Amelia Jane tried to stop – but she toppled and fell over, bang! The toys roared. It was funny to watch Amelia sitting down, plop, glaring at them angrily.

'How dare you laugh at me!' cried Amelia Jane. 'I shall go and learn how to skate in the passage. There is a nice polished floor there – I shall slide beautifully!'

'No, stay here,' said the clown, in alarm. 'You know quite well that somebody may go along that passage and see you, Amelia Jane.'

'Pooh, everyone's in bed,' said Amelia, and this was true, for it was past midnight. 'Anyway, you won't be able to laugh at me there, if I fall down – for none of you dares to come into the passage.'

It was dark in the passage, for only a small light burnt there. Amelia slid out on her soap-skates and began to slide gaily up and down, up and down! The kitchen cat, hearing the noise, came creeping up the stairs, wondering if there was an extra-large-size mouse anywhere about.

He *was* astonished when he saw Amelia. He ran along the passage to see what she had on her feet. Amelia didn't hear him or see him, and she

suddenly bumped right into him.
Crash! She fell over and banged her
head against the bedroom door.

'Sh! Amelia Jane! Sh!' whispered
Tom, putting his head out of the nursery
door. But Amelia Jane wouldn't hush.

She got up angrily and shooed the cat away. But the cat spat and hissed, which scared her a bit.

If Amelia Jane had been sensible she would have run back to the nursery at once, but she was so keen on skating that she once more began to slide up and down, up and down, all along the passage. She didn't hear Nanny's bed creaking. She didn't hear Nanny creeping to the door. She didn't even see Nanny poking her head round the door – no, she went slipping and sliding up and down on the soap, having a perfectly lovely time!

Nanny couldn't make out who or what it was, for the passage was so dark. But she could quite well see something going up and down the passage, skating quickly. She moved to the light switch to put a brighter light on.

Amelia Jane saw her then. Quick as lightning the doll slipped through the nursery door, fell over on the carpet, tore off the bits of soap, and ran to the toy-cupboard. She climbed in on top of the bear and the clown, who were very angry at being walked on.

But nobody dared to say a word! Suppose Nanny had seen what was happening? But when Nanny turned on the big light, all she saw was the kitchen cat sitting calmly by the wall.

'Good gracious,' she said, 'so it was *you* I saw, Puss, skating up and down the passage! What do you mean by doing that in the middle of the night, I should like to know! My goodness, what is the world coming to, when cats take to sliding up and down passages and waking everybody up! Shoo! Shoo!'

She shooed the cat down the stairs, and he disappeared quickly, tail in air, boiling with rage to think that Amelia Jane had slipped off and left him to take the blame.

And in the morning, when Nanny saw the messy bits of soap lying on the carpet, she was crosser than ever.

'Just look at that!' she said to Jane, the cleaner. 'It must be that cat. Slipped and slid down the passage all night long like a mad thing – and then went and tried to eat the soap out of the basin!'

Poor Puss got a scolding! Amelia

Jane laughed at him – but she didn't laugh quite so much when the cat came downstairs and tore her new dress with his sharp claws.

'You'd better not skate any more with the soap, Amelia Jane,' said Tom. 'It's funny to watch you – but if you get other people into trouble it's not fair!'

So that was the end of Amelia Jane skating on the soap. I would have loved to see her, wouldn't you?

Amelia Jane
and the Snow

It was snowing hard. The toys looked
out of the nursery window and watched
the big white snowflakes come floating
down.

'The garden has a new white
carpet,' said the teddy bear.

'Let's send the clockwork clown out
to sweep the dust off it!' said Amelia

Jane, the big naughty doll, with a giggle.

'Don't be silly, Amelia,' said the
clown. 'You do say stupid things.
There's no dust on a snow-carpet!'

'Isn't it pretty!' said the pink
rabbit. 'I'd like to go and burrow in
it!'

'Let's go and play in it!' said the golden-haired doll. 'It would be such fun.'

'Come on, then!' said Amelia Jane. She ran to the door, peeped out, and beckoned the others. 'Nobody's about. We'll slip out of the garden door and go to the bit of garden behind the hedge. Nobody will see us there.'

'Stop a bit, Amelia Jane,' said the clockwork clown. 'Put on a coat. It's very cold outside.'

'Pooh!' said Amelia impatiently. 'Don't be such a baby, Clockwork Clown! I shall be as warm as toast running about. I'm going!'

She ran off down the stairs. But the other toys stayed to put on hats, coats, and scarves. Even the clockwork mouse put a red handkerchief round his neck.

When they got out to the snow they found that Amelia Jane had already made herself a great many snowballs! She danced about as they came, and shouted in glee.

'Let's have a snow-fight! Come on! I've got my snowballs ready. Look out, clown! Look out, pink rabbit!'

The big doll threw a snowball hard. It hit the clown on the head and he fell over, plonk! Amelia Jane giggled. She threw a snowball at the golden-haired doll

and hit her in her middle. The doll gave
a squeal and sat down in the snow.

'Ooh, this is fun!' yelled Amelia.
'Come on, everyone, get some
snowballs ready!'

But nobody could make such big
hard snowballs as Amelia Jane. Amelia
did enjoy herself. She pelted all the toys
with snowballs, hitting them on the
head and the chest and the legs –

anywhere she could.
She was quite a
good shot, and
the toys got
very angry.
'Amelia
Jane! Stop!'
shouted
Tom. 'It isn't

fair. Your snowballs are three times as big as ours, and you make them so hard that they hurt. Stop, I tell you!'

But Amelia Jane wouldn't stop. No, she went on and on – and how she laughed when all the toys turned and ran away from her shower of snowballs!

'Let's leave her alone,' said the clown crossly. 'She's too tiresome for anything.'

'But she'll follow us and go on snowballing us,' said the mouse.

'No, she won't. She's found something else to snowball,' said the teddy bear. 'Look! She's snowballing the kitten!'

So she was. The kitten didn't mind the snowballs at all because she could always dodge them. She pounced on them as they fell, and Amelia Jane laughed to see her. She forgot about the toys.

'What shall we do?' said the golden-haired doll.

'Let's build a nice, round snow-house,' said the clown eagerly. 'It would be such fun to do that. I know how to. You just pile nice hard snow round in a ring and gradually make a round wall higher and higher. Then you make the wall slope inwards till the sides meet, and that's the roof!'

'Oh yes, that would be lovely!' said Tom. 'We could all live in the snow-house then.'

'But we won't let Amelia Jane come in at all,' said the clockwork mouse, getting a little snowball for the wall of the house.

'No, we won't,' said the golden-haired doll. 'It will punish her for throwing such hard snowballs at us.'

The toys worked hard at their snow-house. Soon the wall was quite high. It was a perfectly round wall. It grew higher and higher – and at last, as the toys shaped it to go inwards, the round sides met together and made a rounded roof.

The toys made a dear little doorway at the bottom. They were very excited, for the house was lovely. The clown ran to the pond, cut a square piece of ice, and ran back with it.

'What's that for?' asked the pink rabbit.

'A window, of course!' said the clown. He made a square hole in the side of the house and fitted in the piece of ice. It made a lovely window!

'Now let's go inside and be cosy,' said the golden-haired doll. So they all crowded into the dear little snow-house and sat down. It was lovely.

But just as the clockwork clown was telling a nice story, Amelia Jane came up. The kitten had gone indoors, and Amelia Jane wanted someone else to play with. She had looked and looked for the toys, but as they were in the snow-house she hadn't seen them.

She suddenly saw the house and came running up to it. She peeped inside the window.

'Oh, what a nice little house!' she cried. 'Let me come in, too!'

'No, Amelia Jane!' shouted all the toys. 'You are too big. Besides, we don't want you.'

'But I'm very, very cold,' said Amelia Jane, and certainly she was shivering.

'Well, you should have been sensible and put on your coat and hat as we did!' said the golden-haired doll.

'Oh, *do* let me come in!' begged Amelia, who hated to be left out of anything. 'Oh, do let me!'

'NO, NO, NO!' shouted the toys.

'Well, I'm *coming* in!' said Amelia crossly, and she began to push her way in at the door. A bit of the doorway fell down at once.

'Don't!' cried the clown, in alarm. 'You will break our house!'

'Serve you right!' said naughty Amelia. But the toys really couldn't bear to see their house broken.

'All right, all right, you can come in,' said Tom. 'But wait till we get out, Amelia. You are so big that there isn't room for anyone else when *you're* inside!'

That pleased Amelia very much. She thought it would be lovely to have the house all to herself. She waited until all the toys had squeezed out of the house, and then she went in.

'Oh, it's lovely!' she cried. She pressed her nose to the window and looked out. 'It's lovely! It's a real little house. This shall be mine. You build another one for yourselves, Toys.'

But the toys were tired. They

stared angrily at Amelia Jane.

'You are a very naughty, selfish doll,' shouted the teddy bear. 'First you snowball us till we have to run away. Then you take our house for your own.'

'I'm cold,' said the clown, shivering. 'Let's go and slide on the ice for a bit. Perhaps Amelia will get tired of our house soon and we can have it again.'

So they went off to the pond and left Amelia Jane by herself.

Amelia felt cold. She shivered and shook in the little snow-house. 'I wish there was a fire in this house,' she said to herself, 'then it would be nice and warm. I'll make one! How the toys will stare when they see I have a nice fire to warm myself by! But I shan't let them come in at all!'

She ran to the wood-shed and got some wood. She found some matches there that the gardener used when he lit a bonfire. She ran back to the snow-house. Soon the twigs were crackling loudly.

'What's that noise?' said the clown suddenly. All the toys stopped their sliding and listened. It came from their snow-house.

'Amelia Jane is lighting a fire there!' said Tom. Then the toys looked at one another – and began to giggle. They knew quite well what would happen if anyone lit a fire in a house made of snow! They ran up to watch.

'You can't come in, you can't come in!' shouted Amelia Jane. 'This is my house, and this is my own dear little warm fire! Oh, I'm so cosy! Oh, I'm so warm!'

The toys stood and watched. The fire blazed up as the twigs burnt. There was a red glow inside the little house. It certainly looked very cosy.

Amelia Jane put out her hands and warmed them inside the house.

But something was happening. The fire was melting the house! After all, it was only made of snow! The walls began to drip. The roof began to drip. The bit of ice that was the window disappeared altogether.

Amelia Jane felt the drips on her back and was cross.

'Who's pouring water on me?' she cried. 'Stop it, or I'll be very angry!'

Drip, drip, drip went the snow as it melted all around her. And suddenly the whole house fell in, for the snow was now so soft and melty that it couldn't hold together. The fire went out with a sizzle.

Amelia Jane disappeared, for the

snow fell all over her!

'Oooh! Ow! What's happened?'
yelled Amelia Jane, very frightened. She

kicked about in the wet snow, and first
her hands came out, and then her head.

She sat in the snow and looked around.

'Ha ha! Ho ho ho!' roared the toys. 'It serves you right, Amelia Jane! You took our house – and you lit a fire and melted it – and it fell on top of you! Ha ha! Ho ho ho!'

Amelia Jane began to cry. She was wet through and very cold. She ran back to the nursery, leaving little wet marks all the way. She sat by the fire there and tried to get dry.

And very soon she began to sneeze: 'A-tishooo! A-tishoo!'

'Now I've got a cold!' she said miserably. 'Oh, why do I get naughty? Something nasty always happens to me when I do!'

'Well, just try and remember that,

next time you feel naughty,' said Tom,
giving Amelia his big red handkerchief.

But I don't expect she'll remember
it, do you?

Amelia Jane Goes Mad

Once, when Amelia Jane, that big rascal of a doll, had been good for simply ages, she suddenly got tired of it and went quite mad! Never in her life had she been so naughty and, really, the toys got quite scared of her!

She was quite silly over water. She thought it was the greatest fun to fill the watering-can that belonged to the children, and lie in wait for any toy to come by at night.

She hid behind the curtain and waited till Tom came by. Then she tilted up the little green can and watered him! Goodness, how he jumped!

'It's raining!' he cried, and ran to get his umbrella. But when he put it up, no rain fell at all, and everyone laughed at him.

'It never

rains in the nursery, silly!' said the clockwork clown.

'Well, look at my wet hair,' said Tom, and he shook a shower of drops all over the clown. 'What do you call that if it isn't rain?'

The clockwork clown snorted, and went to visit the clockwork mouse over in the corner. He didn't know that Amelia Jane was hiding behind the scuttle with the watering-can again! Just as he came by, whistling a merry little tune, Amelia tilted up the can – and, pitter-patter! down came the water over the startled clown.

He ran to get the umbrella then – and holding it carefully over him, he went back to the scuttle to find out what the water was. And there, of course, he found Amelia, laughing till the tears ran down her cheeks.

'Give me that watering-can, Amelia Jane,' said the clockwork clown sternly. When he spoke like that, he had to be obeyed, so Amelia meekly gave him the can. But she soon began to look around for some more water to play with.

This time she found a very naughty thing to do. She found that if she stood on a chair by the wash-basin and turned on the tap, she could make the water spurt out all over the room by putting her hand under the tap. And she waited till the golden-haired doll came by, and then spurted the water all over her!

The golden-haired doll was angry,

because the water went on her hair and took out the curl. So she was a straight-haired doll then, and everyone thought she looked most peculiar.

'I shall have to put my hair in curl-papers tonight, and they are so uncomfortable,' sighed the doll. 'Oh, how I wish I could *punish* Amelia Jane!'

Well, the clown climbed up to the basin, and with his strong hands he turned off the two taps so very tightly that not even Amelia Jane could turn them on again. So she couldn't play *that* trick any more.

Never mind! thought Amelia. I shall think of something else! What fun it is to play with water!

Well, she just couldn't get any

water from the taps, and the toys felt safe. But Amelia Jane knew somewhere else to get water. Yes – the goldfish bowl was full of water for the two goldfish to swim in!

The goldfish lived on a table by the wall. Amelia Jane climbed up to the wash-basin and took the sponge from there. It was quite dry. Then she climbed up to the goldfish bowl and looked into the water.

'Can I borrow some of your water?' she asked the fish. And then, without waiting for an answer, she dipped the sponge into the water and made it dripping wet.

Amelia sat on the table and peeped over the edge, waiting for someone to come by. The rabbit and the dog were

having a little
walk together
and were
coming
near.
Amelia
Jane
giggled.
She
waited until
they were just
underneath,
and then she
squeezed the
sponge gently.
Drip-drip-drip,
drop-drop-drop!
Large cold drops of
water fell on to the

158

dog and the rabbit. They were most surprised. They looked up – but Amelia was no longer peeping over the edge of the table, and they could see nothing. They couldn't understand it.

'I'm wet,' said the rabbit, shaking himself.

'And I'm wet too,' said the dog, licking himself. 'Where did it come from?'

'Can't imagine,' said the rabbit. 'Perhaps we are mistaken. Come, let us go on with our ramble.'

So on they went again, and Amelia Jane watched for them to come back near the table once more. Just as they passed, she held out her sponge and squeezed it hard again.

Drip-drip-drip, drop-drop-drop!

Down came the water and soaked the dog and the rabbit. How angry they were!

'My ears are dripping,' said the rabbit.

'My whiskers are soaked,' said the dog. 'Let us tell the clown.'

Well, as soon as they complained to the clown, he knew quite well it must be Amelia Jane up to her water-tricks again, and he called to her very sternly:

'Amelia Jane! Will you stop soaking everyone? It isn't funny, it is very silly, for you will give everyone a dreadful cold. Where are you?'

But Amelia Jane wouldn't answer, though she was aching with trying to stop laughing. The clown was angry, and set out to look for her. He came too near the table and Amelia Jane saw him.

'I can't help it!' she said to herself. 'I must throw this nice wet sponge at him!'

So she threw the sponge at the clown, and it hit him full in the middle. He fell down with a thud, and the sponge dripped wet on him from top to toe. He got up and stared angrily round. But he could *not* see Amelia Jane. She was crouching down on the top of the table again, behind the goldfish bowl.

The clown went to talk to the doll, whose hair was now in curl-papers. The rabbit, the dog, Tom, and the clockwork mouse came too.

'It's time we stopped Amelia Jane,' said the clown. 'What about doing something to *her* with water? That would really be a good punishment!'

'But how can we?' asked the doll with curl-papers. 'If we throw the sponge at her, she'll only throw it back. And you've hidden the can so that she can't get it.'

Everybody thought hard. And then the clockwork mouse had an idea! He was only a small toy, but he sometimes had surprisingly big ideas.

'I know!' he said. 'What about a siphon of soda-water?'

All the toys stared at him as if he were quite mad. '*You* know!' said the mouse. 'The thing that the big people keep in the dining-room, and squirt into a glass when they want a drink. I've seen them. What about getting one of those out of the kitchen where they are stored, and having a squirt at Amelia Jane? If she's so fond of water, she might like a bit of squirting!'

The toys laughed. The clockwork clown and the rabbit went out of the nursery and down the passage to the kitchen to see if they could find a siphon. They found one quite easily in the larder. It was terribly heavy. They had to fetch the dog to help them to carry it back to the nursery.

Amelia Jane had got down from the table and was busy tying a new hair-ribbon in her yellow hair. She was surprised to hear the heavy bumping as the toys carried the siphon in at the door. She turned round and laughed.

'Whatever have you brought that great ugly thing for?' she asked.

'Do you want to know?' said the clown, bringing it right up to her. Before she could answer, the toys pressed on the handle of the siphon, and the soda-water squirted out with a tremendous hissing noise, right into Amelia Jane's surprised face!

Good gracious! She was so startled that she fell over! The toys squealed with delight and squirted her on the ground. She got up and ran away in a dreadful fright. But the toys followed her, and squirted her all the way! Oh dear, oh dear! Poor Amelia, what a shock she got! The siphon made such a noise, and the water soaked her and ran down her neck and quite took her breath away!

'Do you like water so much now?' cried the clown. 'Do you think it is nice to be soaked? Squirt-squirt-squirt! How do you like to be watered, Amelia Jane?'

Well, Amelia certainly did *not* like it! She squealed and screamed and made such a noise that the toys were really afraid she would wake up everyone who was asleep. So they stopped squirting her and quietly took the siphon back to the kitchen.

Poor Amelia Jane! She had to take off all her clothes, even her underwear, and dry them by the fire. Even her body was wet, and she had to dry that too, turning herself round and round all night long! I don't think she will play with water again, somehow!

And nobody in the house could think where all the soda-water out of that siphon had gone to. Amelia Jane isn't likely to tell them, anyhow!

Amelia Jane and the Matches

This is the tale of Amelia Jane and the matches.

Now all boys and girls, unless they are quite old, are warned by their fathers and mothers never to play with matches. And with toys it is just the same. They must never play with matches, in case they get on fire and burn themselves.

But you can guess that Amelia Jane didn't care about any danger! No! If she could get hold of matches you may be sure she would!

There were never any matches left in the nursery, till one day when Jane lit the fire and forgot to put the matches back in her apron pocket, as she usually did.

Jane left the box of matches on the mantelpiece and Amelia Jane saw it first, of course because she was quite the tallest toy in the nursery.

'Oooh!' she said, pointing upwards. 'Matches! If only I could get them!'

'Don't be naughty,' said the clockwork clown at once. 'You know that children and toys must never touch matches.'

'Pooh!' said Amelia Jane rudely.

'Don't pooh at me like that!' said the clockwork clown. 'It's rude.'

'Pooh, pooh, pooh!' said Amelia Jane. So you can guess she was in one of her naughty moods again.

She stood and thought for a minute. Then she remembered how the cowboy doll had taught her to throw a lasso round anything and jerk it near. If only she could make a loop of rope and throw it carefully, she could get those matches down easily.

She ran to the string-box and opened it. The teddy bear saw her. 'If you're thinking of lassoing those matches and getting them down, just let me remind you what happened last time you tried your hand at that!' he said. 'You lassoed the bowl of tadpoles, and got them all down your neck.'

Amelia Jane took no notice. She got out a long piece of string and made a loop-knot at the end. Then she stood beneath the mantelpiece and threw the string neatly upwards, holding one end in her hand.

'Ooooh!' said all the toys in surprise, because, will you believe it, Amelia Jane got the loop right round the box, and it fell almost at her feet when she pulled the string!

'Aren't I clever!' said Amelia proudly.

'No, you're not, you're just lucky,' said the clockwork clown. 'You're not to touch those matches, Amelia Jane.'

'Pooh!' said Amelia, and she opened the box. 'Now, who wants to see me strike a match?'

The toys felt frightened. They knew quite well that matches can set fire to things and burn them. They ran to the toy-cupboard and crept inside, all except the clockwork mouse, and he did badly want to see a match struck.

'I'd like to see some matches struck, please, Amelia,' he said, and he ran nearer.

'Well, you shall see a whole lot struck!' said the big doll. 'The others have all run away, the sillies. You and I will enjoy ourselves!'

Amelia opened the box. She took out a match. She struck it hard on the side of the box. Fizzz-zzz-zzz! The match lit and Amelia Jane held it up in the air, watching the bright flame.

The clockwork mouse liked it very much indeed. He thought it was most exciting.

'Please, please, let me light one too,' he begged.

'Amelia Jane, if you let the mouse strike a match we'll all come out of the cupboard and punish you,' shouted the clockwork clown. 'He's too little to do dangerous things like that.'

'All right, all right!' said Amelia, striking another match. 'I shan't let him. Besides, I want to strike them all myself!'

But before Amelia Jane could strike any more matches there came the sound of steps on the landing outside. The toys flopped down. Amelia ran to the cupboard, throwing the box of matches into a corner. The clockwork mouse ran into the brick-box. So when Jane looked into the nursery, there was no one to be seen at all. Everything was quiet. She had come to put some fresh flowers on the table. Then she dusted round a bit and went downstairs again.

The toys didn't come out for a long time – not until it was night, for they were afraid of being caught.
The first toy that came alive was the clockwork mouse. He saw the box of matches in the corner and was pleased. He ran to them and pushed them along with his nose till he came to a slipper. He popped them into the slipper.

Aha! he thought. Now no one will know where they are, and I can strike as many as I like when the others are not looking!

Now when all the toys came out of the cupboard they looked very stern indeed.

They were angry with Amelia Jane. She had no right to teach the clockwork mouse to play with matches!

The toys sat round Amelia in a circle, and scolded her.

'We shall none of us talk to you for a week,' said the teddy bear.

'We shall not play with you at all,' said the clockwork clown.

'You will not have any of the sweets out of the toy sweet-shop,' said the golden-haired doll.

'And we have hidden your fine new bonnet so that you can't wear it when you go out,' said the pink rabbit.

'Pooh!' said Amelia Jane – but not in a very poohy voice. She was upset. She hated not being talked to or played with. It would be horrid not to have any sweets. And oh, fancy hiding her lovely new bonnet so that she couldn't wear it! Amelia Jane felt like crying. She walked over to the window-seat and sat there, sniffing hard. She was very unhappy.

Suddenly the toys heard a curious noise.

Fizz-zz-zz-zz!

It was the clockwork mouse striking a match all by himself. The toys stared at him in horror. He struck another and squeaked in delight.

But oh, my goodness me, what do you think happened?' His whiskers caught alight! Yes, they really did, and the poor little mouse found himself on fire, with flames burning each side of his little face!

'Sizzle-sizzle!' went his fine whiskers. The mouse squealed in fright and flung away the lighted match. Oh dear – it fell on to an open book and the pages caught alight! The book flamed up, and set light to the brick-box nearby.

'Crackle-crackle!' went the flames merrily. 'Crackle-crackle! We're going to eat the book! We're going to eat the brick-box! Then we'll eat the carpet – and the chairs – and the toy-cupboard – and all the toys – and the whole house! Crackle, crackle, crackle!'

It was dreadful. The toys stared in horror and couldn't move even a paw, they were so frightened. No wonder they had been warned against playing with matches. This was what happened when they disobeyed!

'Eee-eee-eee!' squealed the poor little clockwork mouse, his whiskers burning all away. He ran to and fro in pain and fright. All the toys watched and trembled dreadfully.

And what about that big, naughty doll, Amelia Jane? Yes – she was watching too, her face pale with fright. Poor, poor little mouse – how she wished she hadn't shown him how to strike matches! And oh, that book – and the lovely brick-box! Whatever would happen to them all?

'Well, I began it, so I must try and stop it!' cried Amelia Jane. 'I remember hearing someone say that if anyone got on fire they should be rolled round tightly in a rug to put the flames out. Where, oh, where is a rug?'

'In the dolls' pram!' yelled the teddy bear, who was still too frightened to move.

Amelia Jane ran to the dolls' pram. She snatched up the thick blue rug there and rushed to the little clockwork mouse. She threw the rug all round his little grey body and rolled him up tightly in it, head, tail, and all! She felt the flames trying to burn her hands, and they hurt her, but she didn't stop. She meant to save the little mouse!

The thick rug squashed all the flames out. They died away. There were none left. The clockwork mouse wasn't on fire any more.

But the book and the brick-box were still burning away. Amelia Jane left the mouse and ran to the basin with a jug. She stood on a chair, turned on the tap and filled the jug. Down she climbed and rushed to the brick-box. She threw the water over the flames.

'Sizzle-sizzle!' they said, and died out. They could not go on burning when water was thrown over them. Then Amelia fetched another jug of water and threw it over the burning book.

'Sizzle-sizzle!' said the flames again, and went out. The fire was gone!

The toys came round, looking quite pale. Amelia Jane sat down and began to cry.

'I wish I hadn't touched the matches, I wish I hadn't!' she sobbed.

'I've got no whiskers now!' wept the poor little clockwork mouse. Sure enough, he hadn't – and he did look funny without them. What a noise

Amelia Jane and the mouse made, sobbing together!

'You'll never speak to me or play with me again,' wept Amelia, looking round at the toys. 'I might as well go away from here and never come back.'

'Now listen, Amelia Jane,' said the teddy bear, putting his arm round her. 'You did a very wrong thing, and it has caused a lot of damage – but you have done your best to put it right, and you were brave when all of us were too afraid to do anything.'

'So we will have to forgive you,' said the clown. 'We were angry with you when you were bad, but we think you are brave too, so cheer up.'

'What about the mouse's whiskers, though – and the burnt book and brick-box?' wept Amelia.

'The mouse will have to do without his whiskers,' said Tom. 'The book was very old and torn, so perhaps it won't matter being burnt; and as for the brick-box, it's only the lid that has been burnt, and I can make a new one with the carpenter's set in the toy cupboard. But look at your own hands – and the front of your dress! They are burnt too!'

'It serves me right,' said Amelia Jane. 'I'll put some good ointment on my hands, and I'll have to go about with a burnt bit of dress in front. Oh, I'm so glad you've forgiven me, Toys! I won't be naughty again.'

Well, the toys didn't believe *that*, of course – they knew Amelia Jane too well! But they were soon good friends again, and, secretly, they couldn't help admiring Amelia Jane for putting out the fire so quickly, and saving the little mouse.

'She's like the little girl in the

nursery rhyme,' said the bear to the clown. '*You* know – when she's good she's *very, very* good – but when she's bad she's horrid!'